THE LIBRETTO

GARDNER McFALL

FOREWORD BY SPEIGHT JENKINS

Amelia, a two-act opera in six scenes, with music by Daron Hagen and based on a story by Stephen Wadsworth, was commissioned by Seattle Opera to premiere May 8, 2010.

SEATTLE OPERA

1020 John Street, Seattle, Washington 98109

www.seattleopera.org

UNIVERSITY OF WASHINGTON PRESS

P.O. Box 50096, Seattle, WA 98145 U.S.A.

www.washington.edu/uwpress

ISBN 978-0-295-98939-6 (pbk.; alk. paper)

Library of Congress Control Number: 2009033175

The paper used in this publication is acid-free and 90 percent recycled from at least 50 percent post-consumer waste. It meets the minimum requirements of American National Standard for Information Sciences--Permanence of Paper for Printed Library Materials, ANSI Z39.48-1984. ∞

FOR MY BROTHER,
DODGE McFALL JR.,
TRUE IMAGE OF OUR FATHER

Amelia

THE LIBRETTO

SEATTLE OPERA

in association with

UNIVERSITY OF WASHINGTON PRESS

Seattle and London

CONTENTS

Commissioning a new work is a duty and a privilege given to the general director of an opera company. We must renew our 400-year-old art form if it is to thrive. In the last decade, opera companies both here and abroad have produced more and more new operas, many of which have received generous popular and critical approval. About ten years ago, when the Seattle Opera was on as solid a financial footing as any opera organization can be—the ice on which we were walking was maybe an eighth of an inch thick, not a sixteenth—I set out to accomplish two objectives outside of the normal production of operas: start a Young Artists program and commission an opera.

The Young Artists program celebrated ten years of existence this past season, but *Amelia* is our first commissioned opera. Why the time lag in producing a new work? My problem was finding a composer and a story that I thought would satisfy the public and my own ideals of opera. I have never denied that I am basically a Wagnerian, but I certainly was not looking for a composer who would produce post-Wagnerian music. I do have strong ideas about what makes great opera. I believe, in a very Wagnerian way, that the music comes out of the words, that the words of an opera should be understood by the audience, and that those words should say something relevant—not necessarily tragic or overly dramatic; comedy certainly works. But they must be serious words, serious in the sense of making the listener think.

More important, I wanted a libretto that would serve as the skeleton on which a composer could develop his or her score. The glory of opera is the power of music to enrich words, to give them more than one meaning, or at least intensified meaning. An opera that simply sets the text of a play to music wastes money and time. Why not just produce the play? To answer an obvious challenge, Arrigo Boito in his libretto for *Otello* stripped Shakespeare's *Othello* down to its essentials, knowing that Verdi would amplify every word, and in so doing, Boito created an opera that to me is as powerful as, if not more so than, the original drama. He also added some of those elements unique to opera: large ensembles, strong duets, and choruses.

First must come the composer. I set about finding a composer who had a body of work, including pieces comfortable to the voice, and who had composed the type of music that I wanted for an opera. Once he or she was found, then a subject could be discussed and a librettist chosen to create the text. Since the libretto inspires the music, one might think that composers would get their ideas from writers. Such is not usually the case. Often a composer has an idea that he thinks will inspire him to compose, and he looks for a librettist who is excited by his basic idea.

There is another problem in the creation of an opera, one that didn't seem to affect many composers in the nineteenth century but relates very much to the libretto: gray music. I mean music that only accompanies words and is actually less important. This can happen whether the opera comes from a play or a book; gray music inevitably causes the work to languish seriously. All the money in the world spent for its production and the finest possible singing actors cannot save a piece in which the music does not become memorable. Indeed, the worst possible feeling for an audience member is the sense that the music gets in the way of an interesting story. I also knew that in the history of opera, most of the time the composer chose his or her librettist because there was a synchrony of feeling between them. Richard Strauss and Hugo von Hofmannsthal may not have spent much time together, because Hofmannsthal disliked Strauss's wife, but they communicated totally on both an intellectual and an emotional level.

So how to find the composer? Fortunately there are CDs available of many modern operas, and even without CDs many composers send me (and all the other general directors) the scores of their completed operas, many with piano-accompanied CDs. I thought that, to be fair, I should listen to as many of these operas as possible, then narrow the field down to four composers. I asked Stephen Wadsworth—a good friend, a frequent director at Seattle Opera and the Metropolitan Opera, a distinguished writer and librettist, and a person very knowledgeable in the field—to join me in the search.

We collected maybe thirty operas on CDs and even more scores. This was, I think, in 2002 or early 2003. We listened to them all, studied the scores, and agreed to take notes separately and to come together in six months with some ideas. Together, we had produced some contemporary operas at Seattle Opera, and I knew some of the composers and their works. But I wanted to hear as much as possible before making up my mind. It happened that the works we listened to were mostly American, with a few English composers thrown in. I felt that the work I wanted to commission should be by an American as we are an American company. If a British composer turned out to be my choice, I thought that at least the theme should be American. This is chauvinism, I know, but that was what I wanted to do.

After about nine months, Stephen and I met. Both of us had listened faithfully to all the recordings. I was surprised at how well the works held up on CD. Some of the ones I had seen in the theater seemed better when they were closely studied. I was looking for a composer who walked the narrow line between the kind of post-romantic music that has become increasingly popular since 1990 and a harder-edged, more twentieth-century sound. Like most things in music, it's hard to describe. Samuel Barber? No. Virgil Thomson? No. Arnold Schoenberg? Definitely not. Douglas Moore? No. One knows it when one hears it, but it's almost impossible to describe.

Stephen and I then went over each composer's works. We discussed what they had done, what they were interested in writing about, and whether—and this was vital to me—they wrote singable melodies. We narrowed down the field to four composers, and then Stephen left it up to me. I wrote a letter to the four—this was in, I think, 2004—telling them what I wanted. I felt that the opera should involve the United States either in the closing days of the twentieth century or in the twenty-first century, that it should have the kind of music I have described above, that it should be about two hours in length (I may be a Wagnerian, but I know contemporary operas must be short by nineteenth-century standards, if only because the audience's attention span, trained by television and the movies, requires it), that it could be either a comedy or a drama, but that it should stimulate thought.

Daron Hagen had, as I remember, about six ideas in the first letter, all of which were pertinent to the United States today. Even before writing the letter, I had been very impressed with his last full-length opera, *Shining Brow*, which had its premiere in 1993 in Madison, Wisconsin. Stephen Wadsworth was the director, but Stephen in no way influenced me to choose Daron. He had enjoyed working with Daron but was positive about all four finalists. Daron's response certainly made me want to talk with him. I was instantly taken with his eagerness and his fountain of ideas.

So began a fascinating colloquy. We talked about everything from an opera about Richard Nixon to one on global warming, civil rights, or Native Americans. I honestly can't remember all the subjects, but I do know that maybe because of being the opera company of Seattle, where Boeing for so long has been located, the subject of flight kept coming up. And finally, after a long time and many ideas that seemed to be going nowhere, Daron said one day that he had an idea that dealt with Vietnam and flying. I was immediately interested. At that point the United States had been in Iraq for some two years or more, and the Vietnam War seemed more pertinent than ever, though now distant enough in time that it could be explored without controversy. And though we believed that the Iraq War would be over by the time of the premiere, the subject of Vietnam would mean something to everyone, whatever his or her political persuasion.

I have no recollection of what specific ideas he had, but we pursued the conversation in several calls. Very soon he mentioned that he had a good friend with whom he had worked previously at the Yaddo artists' colony in upstate New York and who was an exceptional poet. He said that she had a personal connection to Vietnam because her father, a navy pilot, had been lost while training for a second tour of duty there, and that she had written many poems about him. Her name was Gardner McFall. He sent me several books to read on the general subject—the latest and most complete biography of Amelia Earhart and several books on flying—but most important a book of Gardner's poems, *The Pilot's Daughter*.

I have to confess that I am not a reader of poetry. I loved Shakespeare and the romantic poets—Byron, Shelley, and Keats—in university, but generally I read prose. Still, Gardner's poems completely overwhelmed me. To start off, their lyrical quality was very musical; they were heartfelt, and they showed that although she had married and had a child, the pain of losing her father had never left her. There were three poems that dealt specifically with losing him. The one that meant the most to me I take the liberty of quoting here:

MISSING

For years I lived with the thought
of his return. I imagined he had ditched
the plane and was living on a distant
island, plotting his way back
with a faithful guide; or, if
he didn't have a guide, he was sending
up a flare in sight of an approaching ship.

Perhaps, having reached an Asian capital,
he was buying gifts for a reunion
that would dwarf the ones before.

He would have exotic stories to tell,
though after a while, the stories
didn't matter or the gifts.

One day I told myself, he is not coming
home, though I had no evidence,
no grave, nothing to say a prayer over.
I knew he was flying among the starry
plankton, detained forever.
But telling myself this was as futile
as when I found a picture of him

sleeping in the ready room,
hands folded across his chest,
exhausted from the sortie he'd flown.
His flight suit was still on,
a jacket collapsed at his feet.
I half thought I could reach out

and wake him, as the unconscious
touches the object of its desire
and makes it live. I have kept
all the doors open in my life
so that he could walk in, unsure
as I've been how to relinquish
what is not there.

It was the last five lines that meant the most to me. Now, thirty years later, she keeps the doors open for him and does not want to relinquish what is not there. The image is so powerful that it stopped me cold. It is not a question of bringing tears to one's eyes. The image can do that, but it could, to my mind, be made even more powerful with music. In other words, it opens the door to thinking and cries out for expansion. I felt then and do now that Gardner McFall was made not only to write poetry but to create poetry that leaves room for more art. Music can expand her poetry; an artist could somehow paint it; a dancer could dance it. What I knew and what was all-important to me was that a singer could sing it, bringing to it even greater feeling than it had as words.

But now what? I liked the idea. I thought that Daron had turned up the ideal librettist, but how could I advise them? The two of them had to discover how to tell the story of the little girl who had lost her father and somehow figured out a way to live without him but still be with him. Daron felt that the story should have links to ancient history, to more modern history, and to the time of composition. I realized when we started talking at length, in particular one day at his club on New York's West Side, that we were embarking on an unusual course. Most operas have a book, a play, a movie, or a myth as a source. An original story, however, has served for some powerful operas—*Aida* and *Die Meistersinger*, are two examples. So we were off but not exactly running. Gardner had to get the ideas down on paper, and they had to be what would stimulate Daron to write the music.

I began to receive interesting scenarios that involved not just the basic story of the little girl who lost her father but also the story of a mythic aviatrix and of Daedalus and Icarus, the father and son of Greek mythology. Trying to escape with his son from the Labyrinth on Crete, Daedalus devised wings that would enable them to fly away. Ignoring his father's warnings, however, Icarus flew too high and too close to the sun. The heat melted the wax that held his wings together, and they fell apart, causing him to crash to his death. Daron and Gardner had lots of wonderful ideas, a fascinating scenario that included much of what is in *Amelia* today, but I thought we needed someone who had worked extensively in the theater and was also a writer to sort out what would work theatrically.

Since Stephen Wadsworth had previously worked with Daron Hagen, and I had asked Stephen to direct the opera, it seemed logical to call on Stephen. He immediately established rapport with Gardner and reestablished his relationship with Daron. He loved Gardner's writing and began to work with the two of them on structuring the book. It was he who believed that there had to be a scene in Vietnam, thus conceivably allowing us to produce the first American opera with some of its text in Vietnamese.

As the idea for the libretto developed, Gardner did an amazing amount of personal research. She visited with members of her father's old squadron, now mostly retired, and made a trip to Vietnam, talking to everyone she could about what it was like during the war, how pilots were treated, what the reaction to them had been. It was a journey she had wanted to make but had not made before. Even though the experience must have been painful, it was, according to what she has told me, both fulfilling and completing. Her reaction to the people she met strongly influenced how she drew the Vietnamese characters. I think the final version of this scene is one of the strongest in both the libretto and the finished opera.

Overall, the libretto became a story of a woman's growth, from the loss of her father to her acceptance of life. She also moves from a rejection of what she believes caused her father's death, namely flying, to an acceptance of his death and of the human spirit's need to transcend the confines of earth. Such a lofty statement, even as I write it, sounds fulsome, but flying does satisfy in many a need to go beyond everyday life, a state to which most humans are attracted. Crucial meetings in shaping the libretto happened in December 2005, when Stephen met with Daron and Gardner. The first act traced the beginning of an interesting arc and held together, but at that point the structure of the second act had to be tightened and strengthened.

Where was the story going? Amelia lost her father; she had vivid dreams of characters long dead; she returned to Vietnam prior to marrying an engineer employed by a company that built airplanes. That she married him—although unstated in the libretto—clearly indicates to me at least that she instinctively knew she had to work out her feelings about her father's death and her reaction to anyone who flew. It was almost inevitable that the man she married would be working not in the commercial end of the airplane business but in the military. This would present the greatest challenge to Amelia. Her pregnancy also was crucial. Into this world that was still so disturbing to her, she was about to bring a child, a girl who might suffer as she did. How could she do it? That was the question of the second act and the crucial question of the whole opera.

Indeed it may be the most important question all of us have to answer. We get married and have children. The world becomes more complex. We as Americans no longer have a country that can claim the kind of hegemony it enjoyed when we were teenagers and similar to what the British had in the nineteenth century. We fight wars that seem to have no end or that don't end the way we think they should. We are increasingly crowded. The environment is threatened. Our position in the world is challenged. Even the value of our money is not what it once was. Yet we still keep bringing children into the world. Politicians promise answers, but nothing happens. The military-industrial complex that former president Dwight D. Eisenhower warned us about almost fifty years ago is even more powerful and more frightening today. So what should we do?

Amelia cannot provide an answer to this question, but, as with all significant art, it poses more questions. This is not a thorny, philosophical text. That kind of work, pace *Tristan und Isolde* and *Parsifal*, generally does not even get one performance, much less meet with success. But by treating the plight of one woman who underwent a great loss as a little girl and who, now pregnant, is determined to break what she feels is a cycle of destruction, Gardner taps into elemental feelings. In Amelia's case, she is perhaps just accepting life for what it is and, realizing that she must, is now ready to move on.

I think the libretto makes for great reading, but to understand fully the depth of Gardner's words and even more important her thoughts and feelings, one must hear Daron Hagen's music. For, like Lorenzo da Ponte, Hugo von Hofmannsthal, Arrigo Boito, or Richard Wagner, to name four of the greatest librettists who ever lived, words without music are only part of the story.

In 2010, when *Amelia* receives its premiere at Seattle Opera, the full meaning of Gardner's extraordinary words will become clear. I am honored to be the general director of the company that will bring this remarkable work of art to life. It is our duty and our joy to make this as great an event as it can be.

Amelia

THE LIBRETTO

DRAMATIS PERSONAE

AMELIA
Mezzo-soprano

DODGE
Tenor
Amelia's father, a U.S. Navy pilot

AMANDA
Mezzo-soprano
Amelia's mother

PAUL
Baritone
Amelia's husband, an aeronautical engineer

THE FLIER
Lyric soprano

HELEN
Dramatic soprano
Amelia's aunt, Dodge's sister.

YOUNG AMELIA
Lyric soprano

DAEDALUS / FATHER
Bass

ICARUS / YOUNG BOY
Tenor

TRANG / NURSE
Lyric soprano

HUY / DOCTOR
Dramatic baritone

INTERPRETER / SECOND DOCTOR
Lyric baritone

COMMANDING OFFICER / GOVERNMENT OFFICIAL
Tenor

CHAPLAIN / GOVERNMENT OFFICIAL / PRIEST
Baritone

NORTH VIETNAMESE ARMY COMMANDER / GRIEF COUNSELOR
Spoken

NORTH VIETNAMESE ARMY SOLDIERS / EXECUTIVES / VILLAGERS
Spoken

* * *

SETTING
The action of the opera takes place in the United States and Vietnam between the years 1965 and 1996.

ACT 1 / SCENE 1

1966, AMERICA, EVENING

YOUNG AMELIA (1965, age 9), on a house porch fronting a yard with a dogwood tree, sings an apostrophe to the stars. She holds her father's cap, on which a commander's insignia is clearly seen. Her mother, AMANDA (1966, age 34), is visible within the house, performing various domestic chores, such as folding clothes and picking up toys, including a Steiff teddy bear, plastic horses, and an airplane. Her father, DODGE (1965, age 35), reads a newspaper. He wears the short-sleeved khaki summer service uniform of a U.S. Navy pilot. His leather flight jacket is thrown over the back of a chair. Throughout the opera, supertitles identify the date and place of the action at the beginning of each scene, as cued in the musical score.

YOUNG AMELIA
Wow—the sky is navy blue . . .
. . . And the stars!

Oh stars, flung wide across the dome,
Heaven is a gown I'd love to wear.
Bathed in your light I'm never alone.
With Ursa Major, Pollux, and Castor—

Hercules stands on the dragon's head,
According to what my father says.
Oh stars, look after my father who flies;
     his name is Dodge.
Please be his safety net and guide.

DODGE rises, tosses the paper on the couch, crosses to the porch, gently taps
YOUNG AMELIA on the shoulder as though to say "Time for bed," recovers his
cap, and returns to the living room. There is no interaction between DODGE
and AMANDA, as they exist in different times.

When I am grown, let me fly, too,
Swift as a windblown leaf or jay,
Clear as the soaring Pleiades,
Unbound by earth and troubles of day;

Starry parade across the dome,
If I had wings I'd fly to you.
I'd ride on the back of Pegasus,
Fixed, but always free to roam.

Anything is possible up in the stars.

DODGE goes out to AMELIA. As they enter the house together and head for

AMELIA's *bedroom, they pass* AMANDA, *who moves out onto the porch to take* AMELIA's *place.*

DODGE
It's time for bed, my angel.

YOUNG AMELIA
I'm not an angel; I'm just a girl!

DODGE
Well then, just a girl,
what did you wish on tonight's first star?

AMANDA *(1966) sees a black sedan with government plates draw slowly up in front of her home.*

YOUNG AMELIA
What I always wish, Daddy—that the stars take care of you.
Please don't go.   AMANDA, *to the car*
                                                                  {Please keep going.}

DODGE
My angel, I'd give anything to stay right here
with you and your mother,
but I have a duty to the men in my squadron.
I'm their commander.

YOUNG AMELIA
But you were already there.
Why should you go back? It isn't fair.

DODGE

It's a matter of *honor.*

> *The car stops.*
> {Don't stop. Drive on.}

YOUNG AMELIA

Where is the Gulf of Tonkin?

DODGE

I'll write to you and your mother every day.
One of the perks of serving there
is that I don't need stamps:
all that I have to do is write the word "FREE"
in the corner of the envelope!

DODGE tickles her, puts his arm around her.

YOUNG AMELIA, *hugging her father*

Oh, Daddy! You know I like to save the stamps!

> {Maybe they're lost.}

DODGE tucks YOUNG AMELIA in.

If I were a bird, I could follow your plane wherever it went.
If I had wings, I'd fly to the stars.
I would travel beside you.
What does it feel like to fly?

> {I'll give them directions.}

DODGE

Imagine a feather pushed up by the wind,
climbing through sea mist and clouds,
propelled into blue.

> {Go away, car. Go away.}

YOUNG AMELIA
Are you ever afraid?

A COMMANDING OFFICER *in full dress uniform and a* CHAPLAIN *in a black suit and clerical collar emerge from the car and silently confer.*

DODGE
Fear is worth feeling to know that sky.

YOUNG AMELIA
Mama says God didn't mean us to fly.

DODGE
Since I was a boy I've wanted to fly.

                    AMANDA
                    {Oh stars, look after my husband
                        who flies . . . }

YOUNG AMELIA
If He did, we'd have wings.

                    (*Twisting the band on her finger*)
DODGE   {. . . Can't help but worry my
God made us dream.   wedding ring.}
All artists dream of flying.
Da Vinci said, "There shall be wings."

YOUNG AMELIA
Why do you fly?

DODGE
Because it's beautiful.
The land and sea are the colors of your quilt;
the rivers are ribbons you could tie in your hair.

The COMMANDING OFFICER *and* CHAPLAIN *start toward the house.*

{Oh stars,

And the stars . . .

look after my husband who flies . . .

YOUNG AMELIA
And you feel free?

DODGE
Free, I feel free as Leonardo's bird.
Whenever you count the stars,
know that I'm thinking of you. Dodge, if I had wings I'd fly to you.}
The two men reach the front door.

CHAPLAIN
Amanda . . .

YOUNG AMELIA
Maybe one day I'll fly too, Daddy.

AMANDA
Oh. Good evening . . . Father.

DODGE, *kissing her forehead*
I'm sure you will, my angel. Good night.

COMMANDING OFFICER
We're sorry to tell you—.
Your husband was leading a mission
last night from Yankee Station.
He was flying over Haiphong.

YOUNG AMELIA, *clutching her father's sleeve, trying to keep him there*
Good night, Daddy.

DODGE
I'll leave the bedroom door ajar.

CHAPLAIN
Dodge is lost in action.

AMANDA slumps, clutching her stomach as though she had just been kicked.

YOUNG AMELIA
Tell me about my name again . . .

AMANDA
Where is he?

DODGE
You're named for a brave woman flier . . .

YOUNG AMELIA
. . . who flew the Atlantic solo . . .

DODGE
. . .and tried to circle the world.

COMMANDING OFFICER
His plane went down in the delta.
His parachute opened.
That's all we know.

CHAPLAIN
We'll keep you apprised of his
status.
Stay near the phone.

YOUNG AMELIA
And she was lost . . .

AMANDA
Find him.

DODGE kisses AMELIA on both cheeks.

COMMANDING OFFICER
We'll do everything we can.

DODGE
. . . and no one knows what became of her.

CHAPLAIN
Try to be strong.

AMANDA, *spoken*
Please *go.*

The COMMANDING OFFICER salutes AMANDA, the CHAPLAIN shares a brief moment with her, and the two men depart. After they are gone, AMANDA reaches into the pocket of her apron and pulls out cigarettes and some matches. She tries several times to strike a spark but is too upset to make it work; she wads the pack of cigarettes and matches in her fist and throws them to the ground, looks around, crosses her arms, and looks down.

DODGE
Dear Amelia, may you sleep,
Enfolded by a perfect dream.
Let angels keep your clever head
Untouched by care or harm.

Find comfort in a dream of stars
Above the earth; dream the moon
Leans close enough for you to touch.
Dream of flight, dream of June,

Whose fireflies across the lawn
Rise unbidden through the trees,
Their invitation on the air:
Climb with us, come, be free.

YOUNG AMELIA has fallen asleep, with DODGE still seated on the edge of her
bed; she has a dream of Amelia Earhart. THE FLIER, in mid-flight, emerges
from the wall, strapped into a suggestion of her cockpit. As she sings, her plane
hovers above YOUNG AMELIA's bed.

THE FLIER
    Cloudy weather, cloudy.
I only felt alive inside the shining hull,
The engine's roar
And run, the thrust of takeoff—
My own Pegasus, my Electra.
    Please take bearing on us and report; we're about two hundred
    Miles out, will whistle into the microphone.
      Noonan, where do you think we are?
      Dawn is almost upon us.
      Then we can sight the island.
Desire brought me here and disregard
For the sensible route. How hot the night is,
The stars all lost in cloud,   **DODGE**, *musing*
                         It's "go" on the Haiphong power
                           plant.
      We crossed the equator three times,
      Didn't we, Noonan? Didn't we? Or is it four?
      It would be four if we're still on course.
The fuel gauge needle falling

While Noonan sleeps on rum.

    Please take bearing on us and report in half an hour.

    I will make noise in the microphone about one hundred miles out.

O trailing wire and transmitter left behind—

Morse code never learned—how could they serve me now?

                                I am leading eight planes and fully
                                      expect

                                   heavy opposition.

    Noonan, it's dawn; the sun is rising.

    The light is blinding.

  We must be on you but cannot hear you.

  Gas is running low; unable to reach you by radio.

  We are flying at an altitude one thousand feet.

Soon, the shudder   AMANDA, *still on the porch*
                                     You *could* have said no, Dodge.

And hush of the sea.

  We are circling but cannot see you . . .

                                   You *could* have said *No*.

  We are running north and south . . .

                                   To have survived eight months on
                                      the line . . .

  Noonan, you told me when you were fifteen,

  You ran away to sea . . .

                                     One tour was enough.

  Well, you are a mariner.

                                   . . . the heat, the stress, the enemy
                                      flak,

                                   the need to be strong.

  Here is the sea—

                                   You *should* have said No!

YOUNG AMELIA (1966), *waking suddenly from her dream*
Ah!

AMANDA *runs into her daughter's room and sits on her bed as* THE FLIER's
plane passes through the wall. Of course, AMANDA *does not see* DODGE.

AMANDA (1966)
I'm right here, sweetheart.   DODGE
                                          Angel, it's just a dream . . .

You were having a bad dream.

YOUNG AMELIA, *clutching her mother's sleeve*
May I call you if I need you?

AMANDA
Of course, sweetheart.

                                          How thankful I am
                                          and how happy you have made me.
                                          My two loves.

AMANDA *kisses* YOUNG AMELIA *on both cheeks, as* DODGE *had earlier.*
YOUNG AMELIA *falls asleep as* DODGE *sings.*

                                          DODGE, *comforting*
                                              YOUNG AMELIA
AMANDA, *comforting*   Sleep, Amelia, sleep, my star;
    YOUNG AMELIA
Find comfort in a dream of stars;

                                          If anything you need, just call.

Arcturus gleams the brightest of all.

We're in the other room, not
far.

Nothing to fear,
I'll leave the bedroom door ajar.   I'll leave the bedroom door ajar.

*Both parents remain on the bed for awhile as the orchestral transition plays.
Presently, DODGE (1965) gets up and exits through the wall. AMANDA (1966)
watches YOUNG AMELIA (1966) sleep, then buries her head in her hands, as
the lights fade.*

ACT 1 / SCENE 2

Possibly the same house. AMELIA *and her husband,* PAUL, *are lying in bed, asleep. A very pregnant (8–9 months)* AMELIA *dreams of* ICARUS *and his father,* DAEDALUS, *who sit on stools in the room. Each toils over a huge feather wing. They are, like* THE FLIER, *the product of* AMELIA's *dreams, artifacts of her poetic memory. Accordingly, neither pair of characters takes notice of the other.*

DAEDALUS
Son!

ICARUS
Father, we must escape soon.
And we will—we'll fly away,
borne on feathers and wax.

(*Admonishing*)
Icarus.

Father.

Son.

AMELIA, *awakening with a start*
Daddy!

PAUL
No, my angel, it's your husband.   AMELIA
                                          Paul . . .
Hope you slept well. Having lots of dreams?

AMELIA, *reaching to stroke his face*
Millions!

PAUL
How do you feel?   ICARUS, *acknowledging* DAEDALUS
                                    We'll fly away, we'll escape.

AMELIA, *wry*
It's too early to know . . . *coffee*, please.
                                    We'll fly away . . .

PAUL, *smiling*
Ah, yes . . .

The telephone rings. PAUL *reaches clumsily over her to answer it. He is
somewhat secretive on the telephone.* AMELIA *gets up while* PAUL *speaks,
pulls on her robe, then leans back on the bed.*

PAUL, *into the phone*
Yes. Yes. No hurry.
Uhn-uhn. This is a good time.
Sure enough . . . um . . .
we'll go over the designs this afternoon.

Uh-huh. Yes. Okay.
Okay.

PAUL hangs up the phone, smiling.

AMELIA
You can't talk about it, right?

PAUL
Honey, you know I can't . . .
(*Changing the subject*)
Have you seen the doctor since Thursday?

AMELIA
Yes, I have, Paul.

PAUL
So?

AMELIA
He says everything's fine.
But I had that dream again just now.

PAUL
What was it about?

AMELIA
About the boy who flew too near the
     sun,

                        PAUL
                        Right. Icarus.

trying to escape the labyrinth, and then—
you know how dreams are—it shifted,
and I was coming home.
Our lawn was covered with dead blue jays.
Their wings were electric blue—
a Technicolor blue, like the sea the boy falls into—
and I thought, God, I'll never be able
to bury them all.

PAUL rises from bed and begins dressing.

PAUL
That dream again?

AMELIA
Uh-huh.

ICARUS
A dream of flying.

PAUL
That dream is about rebirth.

A dream of feathers and wax.

AMELIA, *gazing off*
Oh, really? I've never heard that.

PAUL
You miss your mother.

AMELIA
More, more, than I can say,

Swift, swift as a windblown leaf or
jay,

and especially now, with a baby on the way.

> unbound by earth and troubles of
> day.

What's this plane, Paul,
that you're working on?

PAUL
Oh, no, you don't.
That's not really what you want to know.
Is it?

> (*Agitated*)
> As though these wings could work!

AMELIA

> (*Throws the wings down*)

I sometimes wonder why we ever thought
to bring a baby into
such a world of pain and loss.

> **DAEDALUS**
> You tried them, and you fell back.
> Remember, the wax can crack.

PAUL
Pain and joy:
Darling, they're intertwined.

AMELIA
About the plane . . .

> Patience, Icarus!

PAUL, *kissing her on the cheek, a familiar deflection*
Nice weather we're having.

AMELIA pushes his shoulder in an attitude of "oh, stop," then moves to the vanity to brush her hair. PAUL continues dressing for work.

ICARUS
What does it feel like to fly?

DAEDALUS
Imagine a feather pushed up by the
    wind,
climbing through sea mist and
    clouds.

Are you ever afraid?

You must fly straight;

Ah!

you must take care;

Father, I . . . Father . . .

we'll make a pact . . .

Feathers . . .

. . . I know, and wax.
Don't fly near the . . .

. . . water.

AMELIA
I can't bear secrets, Paul.
I have to know why.
Now that Mama is dead,
I have to know what happened to
    my father.

ICARUS
I know the feathers can't get wet.

DAEDALUS
And don't fly too near the sun.

I have to know, Paul,
about the plane;

ICARUS
Don't worry . . .

I have to know . . .

      . . . the wax won't melt.

. . . about my father.

      DAEDALUS
      Promise me.

      ICARUS
      I know what I'm doing.

I have to know . . .
. . . what you are doing.

      DAEDALUS
      Promise me.

PAUL
Not every flier flies too near the sun.

      AMELIA
      Why did that boy approach the sun?

Not every flier falls to earth.

      I'd like to see a *man* give birth.

(*Places his hand on her belly*)
I can help you overcome your fear.

      I have this fear that harm
      will touch the ones we love . . .
      the ones *I* love.

Out of every death there comes rebirth.

      (*Gently removing his hand*)
      Nothing is certain.

Darling, we'll make a pact.

      Life is fragile.
      Leave the door open, Paul.

Why not call your aunt?

                                    Aunt Helen. Huh. That's a good
                                    idea.

You love it when she's here.

                                    I love you.

(*Picking up his briefcase, preparing to leave*)

Angel, I love you.   (*Wry, again*)

                                    Leave the door open.

                                    Daddy might come back.

(*Laughing, kissing her on the cheek and exiting*)

Yes, I know.

AMELIA

Why think of the blue canary I had
At six? While I was cleaning her cage,
She escaped and flew through the window,
Lost to her fate. Another time,

A sparrow crashed into our porch.
It had taken the glass for space.
The moment that a bird takes flight, it can die,
And yet the house finch makes

Her nest beneath the eaves.
She tends her nest until her chicks are grown
Or big enough to leave.
How do they learn to fly—and why?

There is no choice.
       That is nature's way
             Of telling us:

Don't be afraid.

I am afraid.

AMELIA, still in her dressing gown, remembers her mother, AMANDA, who comes through the wall.

AMANDA (1966)
Sweetheart, come finish your breakfast.
You'll be late for school.

> AMELIA, *assuming the role of herself in 1966*
>
> Oh, Mama, I'm so tired.

Did you finish your essay on Edna St. Vincent Millay?

> Yes, I did—it's even a page longer than it has to be.

Did you memorize the poem?

> (*Reciting*)
> "O world, I cannot hold thee close enough!

Sweetheart.
(*Reaching to put her arm around AMELIA*)
My darling,
I have something to tell you.
Last night I got some news about Daddy.

> Thy winds, thy wide grey skies . . ."

> What is it?

He's missing.

> (*After a beat, angry*)
> It's just a dream.
> You were having a bad dream.

AMELIA grabs her books and runs offstage. AMANDA tries to hold her back, then calls out to her.

Leave the door open, sweetheart!

Offstage, a door slams.

AMANDA
So what would you say to her now, Dodge?

        ICARUS, *finishing the wing*
        They'll remember us, Father.

That pain and joy are intertwined?   **DAEDALUS**, *to his son*
                        Yes, yes, it's true.

Dodge, you promised me you'd fly . . .
        I'm flying away,

. . . back to me,

                Stay with me,
                . . . Son.

      . . . Father.

. . . Husband.

There is a brief beat of silence as DAEDALUS accepts the inevitable and rises to his feet.

                Alright.
    (Standing)   Let's go.
    Risky.

                A dream of flying . . .

Who invented flying? And *why*?

The lights fade. The three stand there, uncertain.

ACT 1 / SCENE 3

The lights slowly rise, revealing a small North Vietnamese village sometime in 1985. There is a low, brick-walled square, with the entrance to a communal house, framed by Chinese dragon sculptures, and individual dwellings made of mud (or wood) and red-tile roofs, over which pink-flowered vines hang to one side. "Chú ý: trẻ em" *is written in bold white letters on the wall; it means* "Pay attention: look out for the children." *A North Vietnamese flag, red with a gold star, is visible on a makeshift pole. The square itself is carpeted with blond rice stalks put out for drying. Rice paddies are seen in the distance, steel-colored water buffalo, perhaps some brown cows, and, distinctly, the wreckage of an A-4 Skyhawk clearly marked with American naval insignia, its single wing protruding from the ground at an impossible angle. Center stands the hutlike home of* TRANG *(pronounced "Chang") (55) and* HUY *(pronounced "Hwe") (60). Three steps lead up to a door through which a large flat bamboo platform for sleeping can be seen to the right, and a wooden table and benches to the left. In the middle stands an ancestral altar, draped in red, with burning incense and photographs of deceased family members.*

AMANDA (53) and AMELIA (29) enter, accompanied by an INTERPRETER.

AMANDA
They tell me everything's changed.

AMELIA
These are the fields he looked at;
it's the same sky.

TRANG and HUY enter from the hut, bowing slightly. They wear blowsy brown trousers and jewel-necked tunics that button up the front. TRANG wears a conical hat. AMELIA and AMANDA bow awkwardly.

HUY
Xin chào.

INTERPRETER
Welcome.

AMELIA
Hello.

AMANDA
Thank you.

HUY
Mọi người dùng một chút rượu nếp nhé?

INTERPRETER
Would you like some rice wine?

AMANDA
Thank you, no.

INTERPRETER
Ồ không, xin cảm ơn.

AMELIA
Don't go to any trouble.

INTERPRETER
Không nên làm phiền họ.

TRANG offers lotus flowers to AMELIA and AMANDA.

The lotus is the flower of our country.

AMELIA
It's very beautiful.

INTERPRETER
Bó hoa sen thật đẹp.

AMANDA
It's absolutely beautiful.

INTERPRETER
Vâng, bó hoa sen này rất đẹp.

TRANG bows. There is a long, awkward silence.

AMANDA
We were so glad to get their letter.

INTERPRETER
Họ rất mừng khi nhận được thư của ông bà.

AMELIA
We were amazed . . .

INTERPRETER
Họ vô cùng ngạc nhiên . . .

AMELIA
. . . to get it after all this time.

INTERPRETER
Đã có thông tin về người than của mình sau nhiều thời gian.

HUY and TRANG nod yes. Another awkward silence.

AMELIA
You wrote that you knew something.

INTERPRETER, *nodding yes, he understands*
Cô ấy muốn biết về người cha của mình.

TRANG and HUY confer for a moment.

TRANG
Ông ây là một người tốt.

INTERPRETER
He was a good man.

HUY, *pointing off left*
Máy bay của ông ấy bị bắn rơi ở đằng kia.

INTERPRETER
He was shot down over there.

Scattered sounds of M-1 semiautomatic carbines firing from off left. DODGE
*hurtles onstage, covered in mud, dragging his parachute. Through the ripped
shoulder of his flight suit we see his blood-drenched T-shirt and a deep gash
oozing blood. The shoulder is dislocated. There are shouts in Vietnamese.*
DODGE *looks around wildly for a place to hide his gear. He conceals it just
beyond the door of the hut before collapsing within. The dialogue overlaps
and occurs at the same time as the stage action.*

HUY
Ông ấy bị thương.

INTERPRETER
Your father was hurt.

AMELIA
Badly?

HUY
Vào vai.

INTERPRETER
His shoulder.

HUY
Chúng tôi nghe thấy tiếng động lạ bên ngoài.

NVA SOLDIER, *shouted, gesturing to another soldier, off*
Hãy nhìn về phía kia!

INTERPRETER
We heard something outside.

HUY
Chúng tôi dã tìm thấy ông ấy.

INTERPRETER
We found him.

HUY
Chúng tôi không biết phải làm gì.

INTERPRETER
We didn't know what to do.

DODGE, *a wail*
Xin hãy giúp tôi!

INTERPRETER
Help me!

The sound of strafing fire. VILLAGERS *(perhaps eight adults and a dozen children) race pell-mell as the first* NVA SOLDIER *enters, wearing an olive-green uniform, a short-sleeve green shirt and same color pants, a belt, and a hat, carrying an automatic weapon. He is followed by a handful of others. Three rush toward* TRANG *and* HUY, *as others secure the little square and herd the* VILLAGERS *toward the hut while looking up at the receding plane(s).*

NVA COMMANDER, *to* HUY, *brandishing his weapon*
Tên Mỹ đó đậu?

INTERPRETER
Where is the American?

The VILLAGERS *are still. No one knows.*

NVA COMMANDER
Hắn là tên giặc lái máy bay!

INTERPRETER
He's an air pirate.

The NVA COMMANDER *fires a round from his pistol into the air. The* VILLAGERS *cling together.*

AMELIA, *spoken*
You didn't say anything?

INTERPRETER, *spoken*
Ông bà không nói gi chứ?

34

HUY, *spoken*
Chúng tôi không nói gì.

INTERPRETER, *sung*
No.

NVA COMMANDER
Ai là người giúp đỡ kẻ thù?

INTERPRETER
Who is aiding the enemy?

The NVA COMMANDER *motions to his men to search the little square and hut.*

NVA SOLDIERS, *variously, looking for* DODGE.
Giết hắn đi!

HUY
Họ nói: giết hắn đi!

INTERPRETER
Kill him!

DODGE *emerges from the hut. The* NVA SOLDIERS *grab him and drag him to the wall.*

NVA SOLDIERS, *variously*
Tên giặc mỹ!

HUY

Họ gọi ông ấy là tên giặc lái.

INTERPRETER

They called him an air pirate.

The NVA SOLDIERS *throw* DODGE *against the wall.*

NVA SOLDIERS, *variously*

Tội phạm chiến tranh!

HUY

Họ nói: Tội phạm chiến tranh.

INTERPRETER

War criminal!

TRANG

Họ gọi ông ấy là tội phạm chiến tranh.

The soldiers kick DODGE.

NVA SOLDIERS, *variously*

Hãy thú tội đi!

INTERPRETER

Confess your guilt!

HUY

Họ bảo ông ấy phải thú tội.

NVA COMMANDER
Nhiệm vụ của mày là gì?!

INTERPRETER
What is your mission?

DODGE does not respond.

AMELIA
And still you said nothing?

INTERPRETER
Và ông bà vẫn im chứ?

HUY
Chúng tôi vẫn không nói gì.

INTERPRETER
Nothing.

NVA COMMANDER
Nhiệm vụ của mày là gì?!

INTERPRETER
What is your mission?

NVA SOLDIERS, *variously*
Tội phạm chiến tranh!

INTERPRETER
War criminal!

NVA SOLDIERS, *variously*
Hãy thú tội đi!

INTERPRETER
Confess your guilt!

The NVA COMMANDER *pistol-whips* DODGE.

DODGE, *otherworldly*
I have faith in God.

NVA COMMANDER
Mục tiêu bỏ bom cua mày là gì?

INTERPRETER
What are your targets?

DODGE
I have faith in my country.
I will do my duty.

NVA COMMANDER
Hãy khai ra!

INTERPRETER
Speak!

The NVA COMMANDER *pulls a* YOUNG GIRL *from among the cowed*
VILLAGERS *and throws her against the wall with* DODGE. *He turns the*
semiautomatic away from DODGE *and places it to the head of the girl.*
DODGE *registers the threat.*

NVA COMMANDER
Hãy khai đi! Đùng buộc tội phải bắn nó!

INTERPRETER
Confess . . . or you force me to shoot her!

AMANDA *drops the flower and falls to her knees. The* NVA COMMANDER
shoots the girl and signals his men to shoot DODGE. *Both collapse against*
the wall and lie motionless. The VILLAGERS *jerk back and are disbanded by*
the NVA SOLDIERS, *including the* NVA COMMANDER. *All of the* SOLDIERS
go upstage.

AMELIA, *to* TRANG
Why did you wait so long to write to us?

INTERPRETER
Tai sao ông bà gửi lá thư cho họ?

HUY
Bởi vì bé gái ấy là con đẻ của chúng tôi.

INTERPRETER
Because the girl was our daughter.

TRANG *falls against* HUY. AMANDA'*s hand shoots out to take* AMELIA'*s hand.*

AMELIA
Why did you write to us at all?

INTERPRETER
Tại sao ông bà quan tâm viết thư cho chúng tôi?

DODGE *stirs, pulls his upper body up, looks at his shattered legs, and scans the little square for* NVA SOLDIERS. *He sees the dead* YOUNG GIRL, *pulls himself over to her, reaches across her body to close her eyes with his fingers, kisses her forehead, sees* TRANG *and* HUY, *searches in his pocket, extracts a small photo and reaches with it toward* TRANG, *who takes it and looks at it. Upstage, as the huts are being searched, snatches of conversation in Vietnamese filter on from the departing* NVA SOLDIERS *as the scene continues.*

DODGE, *pointing to the photo and to himself*
Con gái . . .

INTERPRETER
Daughter.

TRANG
Chúng tôi gửi thư vì ông ấy là một người tốt.

INTERPRETER
We wrote to you because . . .

HUY
Ông ấy thật cao thượng.

INTERPRETER
. . . because he was good.

HUY, *struggling for the words*
He . . . *good.*

INTERPRETER
He was noble.

DODGE looks hurriedly around, then extracts an envelope. He reaches with it toward TRANG but drops it when he hears voices of NVA SOLDIERS approaching. TRANG pockets the photo quickly, and HUY covers the letter with his foot as two soldiers suddenly appear; they lift DODGE by the arms and drag him off left. TRANG and HUY back away from the letter, looking at it. AMELIA is left standing; AMANDA is kneeling; HUY and TRANG face them, the body of the YOUNG GIRL in a heap by the wall. TRANG climbs the steps, enters the hut, and takes a photo off the altar.

INTERPRETER, EXPLAINING, AS *TRANG approaches the altar*
We keep pictures of our ancestors on the altar.

TRANG returns and presents the snapshot to AMELIA, who looks at it.

AMELIA
That was my favorite sweater.

AMANDA
And that paper?

INTERPRETER, *pointing to the letter on the ground*
Và tờ giấy đó?

HUY
Là một bức thư gửi gia đình ông ấy.

INTERPRETER
A letter for you.

AMANDA, *anguished*
Do you have it?

TRANG
Chúng tôi đã đốt nó rồi.

INTERPRETER
We burned it.

TRANG
Chúng tôi vô cùng căm giận.

INTERPRETER
We were very angry.

The lights slowly fade and the tableau is held as VILLAGERS *are perceived to be continuing an ordinary day's labor—walking over rice to separate it from straw, bundling it, and stacking it against a wall.*

END OF ACT 1

ACT 2 / SCENE 1

1996, AMERICA, AFTERNOON

A large meeting is breaking up at PAUL's *office, a modern metal-and-glass space with huge picture windows framing the sky. As the scene progresses, the sky changes from blue to dusk; stars begin to appear at the very end. Gradually, all of the* EXECUTIVES *filter out, leaving* PAUL *with only a few people, including two* GOVERNMENT OFFICIALS, *portrayed by the same actors who played the officials who brought the news about* DODGE's *disappearance in act 1, scene 1. As they are about to take their leave,* AMELIA, *at term, arrives suddenly, a bit distraught; she makes eye contact with them and forces her way between them as she works her way across the room to her husband.*

AMELIA, *to the* OFFICIALS
I need to speak to my husband.

No one moves.

Alone.

The GOVERNMENT OFFICIALS *look to* PAUL.

Now.

The GOVERNMENT OFFICIALS *leave.*

                              PAUL
                              Are you all right?
                              Are you okay?
I've been thinking about what we said this morning.
Whatever this plane is you're building, you have to stop it.
                              Darling, this is my work.
Well, you have to stop it.

                              It's not that simple.

(*Looking out the window*)
Where have I heard that before?
I have a feeling we're tempting fate.
This plane—what is it, a bomber?   (*Stiffening*)
                              You don't know that, Amelia.

So it *is* a bomber.

                              That's not what I said.

Your bomber
will bring us the worst sort of luck.

                              That's in the past.
The past taught me airplanes are bad.

                              All airplanes? That's ridiculous.
I don't want our future to echo my past.

                              How could it?
I just want closure and peace.

Now is our chance to transform the
    past.
(*Tries another tack*)
You're simply afraid.

There's just so much we simply can't know.

Yes, I know.

Why don't you understand?

Try to explain to me . . .

I've tried making peace with the past.

The past is the past.
Let go of it. Come on,
why can't you grasp . . .

I knew as a child my father wasn't
coming home.

. . . I come home. I'm your anchor,
    your rock.
(*Aside*)
What do I come home to?
You and a ghost.

And when they said he was lost,
I prayed he'd be found.
It gave me hope.

I know you hurt, but we need to
    move on.
You went to Hanoi,
and you know now what there is to
    know.

What's there to know?
What good did it do? We didn't even
    find out.

Amelia, you found out a lot.

Same old questions—did he die?

We have to assume he died.

More important—*why*?

The sky outside has darkened perceptibly; golden, late afternoon sunlight streams in through the windows.

"All wars are boyish, and are fought
by boys—"   Who said that?

And what is it for—what good did it do?

How will I explain to our child what happened?
I lost my father like a thimble or jack—
and for what? No war is worth that.
From inside the hangar I watched him
walk to his plane. He grew smaller and smaller
like a jet that becomes a dot in the sky.
I should have held him tighter.
I should have begged him to stay.

                                    But you were just a kid.
When he died, I told myself
the worst that could happen had happened.
And nothing more would touch me that way.

A child should know her father and mother,
beginning to end, live in a nice, big house
like in a child's drawing, coming in, going out.
When I think of all he missed dying young.
He'll never push our child in a swing.
And what I missed with him gone—the lost conversations.
Everyone said, "You're the image of your father."

Look, I'm older than he was—
what if I die giving birth?

More people die crossing the street,

It's risky,

than flying in a plane . . .

though that never comes up in Lamaze.

. . . or giving birth.

And yet beneath all this—
buried like a bulb in the dirt
is my fear: a baby. Oh no—not another thing
to love.

Amelia.

See and feel how it hurts!

Amelia.

I loved him better than life.
I lost my world.

(*Reaches for her, but she pulls away*)
Amelia!

How, how can I bear . . . the risk?

The sky outside has turned a deep shade of navy blue, as in act 1, scene 1. Tiny stars have begun to emerge.

Oh, the helplessness
that blood ties bring:
Love equals loss.

"Imagine a feather pushed up by the wind,
climbing through sea mist and clouds . . ."

I remember his words:
"Fear is worth feeling."

(*Seems to notice the sky for the first time and is clearly on the verge of fainting*)

You traded us for your love of the sky . . . how could you? How could you do that? . . . You valued honor more than you did me . . . how could you? How could you die? You died before I could take you off the pedestal . . . Daddy, why did you die? I needed you more than your squadron did. I needed you! "Starry parade, if I had wings I'd fly to you . . . Anything is possible up in the stars . . ." So many stars . . . Carry me there, Pegasus . . . carry me, Daddy . . . so many stars!

AMELIA *collapses.* PAUL *rushes to her side, reaches for his cell phone, dials 9-1-1.*

PAUL, *calling off as the call goes through*
Someone, help!

The lights quickly dim as people begin entering the room.

ACT 2 / SCENE 2

Stage left, a YOUNG BOY *who has fallen from a great height (portrayed by the actor who played* ICARUS*) is revealed resting fitfully in a bed in a hospital room, flanked on one side by a heart monitor and on the other by his* FATHER *(portrayed by the actor who played* DAEDALUS*), who sits on the edge of the bed holding his son's hand. Stage right, on the other side of a hanging hospital curtain,* AMELIA*, asleep, lies in another bed, connected to a monitor that is tracking the heartbeat of her baby;* PAUL *sits on the edge of the bed, holding her hand.* PAUL *has clearly spent the night on a nearby recliner, on which a hospital blanket lies rumpled. A* NURSE *(portrayed by the actor who played* TRANG*) comes in and checks the* YOUNG BOY*'s monitor, then his chart, which she hangs at the foot of the bed. She seats herself on a small chair next to the boy's bed. A* DOCTOR *(portrayed by the actor who played* HUY*) enters with test results, startling* PAUL*.*

PAUL

How is she doing?

DOCTOR

She's unconscious.

She's stable.

The baby is absolutely fine.

I think a C-section would be best.

We don't know why she's unconscious.

(*Reading the chart*)

You know that you're having a girl.

                                        Yes . . .

Lucky man. Girls love their fathers . . .

                                        Will she wake up, Doctor?

(*Another beat*)

Go get some fresh air.

Get some breakfast.

PAUL exits. The DOCTOR *exits; we follow him as he crosses past the* YOUNG
BOY's *bed and is flagged down by the* FATHER.

FATHER

Doctor, can you help me?   **DOCTOR**

                                      This isn't my case, but let me see.

The DOCTOR *stops, looks at the* YOUNG BOY's *chart.*

                                      He fell.

Yes.

                                      I'm sorry.

Can he hear us?

                                      (*Reading*)

                                      "Delirious. Unresponsive."

                                      We don't know.

He squeezed my hand;
I think he can hear me.

I'll page his doctor.
I don't know this case.

NURSE, *to the* FATHER
The doctor will be here soon.

The NURSE *gets up, crosses to* AMELIA, *and makes notes on her chart.* HELEN
enters briskly, still clad in an overcoat and scarf.

NURSE
Excuse me. May I help you?

HELEN
I'm her aunt.
I've just flown in.
What's going on?

She fell.

I know.

Oh.
She's been unconscious for three days.

The gravity hits HELEN. *She looks at* AMELIA.

Could I see her chart?
"Three days . . ."

I've a feeling the baby will come soon.

I think you're right.
I'm a midwife.

The NURSE *gives* HELEN *the chart;* HELEN *examines it.*

Where's her husband?

He took a break.

(*Looking at* AMELIA)
She is my brother's child.
What are her chances?

They don't know.
They don't know where she is.

(*To* AMELIA)
Oh, listen, my darling:

The NURSE *moves away to the* YOUNG BOY'S *room.*

If I had wings I'd fly to you.

HELEN *overhears the* YOUNG BOY'S *cry. The* NURSE *crosses to the* YOUNG BOY'S *bed.* HELEN *removes her coat, places it on the chair, straightens the sheets, and sings to* AMELIA *as she strokes her hair. In due course, a* SECOND DOCTOR *(portrayed by the actor who played the* INTERPRETER*) enters. During the following exchange between the* FATHER *and his son, there is a wordless exchange between the* DOCTOR *and the* NURSE*, who prepares an injection.*

YOUNG BOY, *sudden, reliving his fall*
Father!

FATHER
Right here, son.

FATHER
Father!

HELEN
When you were born, your father told me:

FATHER
Son . . .

YOUNG BOY, *happy now*
I'm flying, Father! I'm flying!

FATHER
You're here. With me.

HELEN
"Now we're really a family."

YOUNG BOY, *becoming restless, tormented*
Flying away!

FATHER
Nurse!

HELEN
I used to . . .

FATHER
What's happening?

HELEN
. . . push you on the swing.

YOUNG BOY, *terrified*
Flying! Flying!

NURSE, *reading the boy's chart*
"Morphine." He's hallucinating.

HELEN
What was that rhyme . . .

YOUNG BOY
Flying!

FATHER
Hallucinating?

HELEN
. . . you loved to sing?

YOUNG BOY
I have to go now.

FATHER
What's that, son?

HELEN
"Up in the air . . ."

NURSE
"Ativan."

YOUNG BOY
Father?

HELEN
". . . I go flying again."

NURSE
The doctor could increase the dosage.

YOUNG BOY
I have to get out of here.

HELEN
"Up in the air . . ."

FATHER, *to the* **NURSE**
What's that?

YOUNG BOY
Daddy, are you with me?

NURSE, *to the* **FATHER**, *giving the injection*
This will calm him down.

HELEN
". . . and down."

YOUNG BOY
Father?!

FATHER
Son!

The YOUNG BOY *relaxes almost immediately. The* YOUNG BOY'S *cry silences* HELEN, *who rises from* AMELIA'S *bed and moves toward the* YOUNG BOY'S *room to listen.*

FATHER
I am with you.
(*To the* NURSE)
Thank you.
(*To the* SECOND DOCTOR)
What will happen to him?

SECOND DOCTOR
Sir, your son is . . . his injuries are life-threatening.
I think . . . there's nothing that I can do for him.
But we'll try to make him comfortable.

HELEN *sinks to her knees.*

HELEN, *praying*
Oh stars, flung wide across the dome,
If only you could guide her home
Or your Creator's hand might bend
To bring my brother's daughter back.
Oh hear this prayer: extend her days.
For this I'll give God endless praise.

(*To* AMELIA)
Wherever you're trapped, spring free.
Become who you were meant to be—
Witness to mystery, death, and love.
Bring forth life.
I see your father still in you—
You'll find him in your baby too.

The SECOND DOCTOR *briefly touches the* FATHER *on the shoulder as he goes.*
DODGE *enters, wearing his naval dress whites and air medals. He removes his
cap as he approaches* AMELIA's *bed and awakens her by tenderly taking her
hand.* AMELIA *opens her eyes and smiles.*

DODGE
Con gai.

The door was ajar.

AMELIA
Daddy. You're here . . .

. . . just like I dreamed, only in my
    dreams you didn't speak; you
    stood under the dogwood tree
    in the yard.

You're going to have a baby.

Am I?

You are.

We haven't seen each other in a
    while.

True.

So much has happened.
Daddy, I'm afraid.

HELEN
Of course you're nervous . . .

FATHER, *to the NURSE,*
who has just brought him a cup of coffee
Thank you.

but, imagine:

AMELIA, *to DODGE*
I'm not conscious.

NURSE, *to FATHER*
You're welcome.

DODGE, *to AMELIA*
Yes, I know.

Millions of babies are born each day.
This is your moment to shine, so,
honey, wake up.

HELEN rises and looks toward the YOUNG BOY's bed.

AMELIA, *to DODGE*
What is it like?

DODGE
Being a parent?

AMELIA
No, Daddy. Being dead.

DODGE laughs ruefully.

I was thinking of joining you. I miss you.

DODGE
It's not like anything I knew
When living on the earth with you.
It's sun and rain, less and more;
Time stops, and yet lies in store.
All human failure dissipates.

AMELIA
That's what I was hoping.

DODGE chuckles lightly. HELEN crosses past the YOUNG BOY's bed.

FATHER, *to HELEN*
Excuse me. . .

HELEN, *to the FATHER*
Yes?

AMELIA, *to DODGE*
You make it sound like a perfect dream
the dreamer has but cannot relate . . .

FATHER, *to HELEN*
Do you think he'll live?

DODGE
But love abides; love shames death.

AMELIA
A full-blown galaxy of stars,
Forever fixed but free to roam,
Suspended in the infinite
Where everything is possible.

HELEN, *to the* FATHER
I hope he lives.

HELEN moves to a chair near the FATHER *and sits.*

DODGE
Though human failure dissipates,
So does risk and new success.
You never feel the distance close
Between what you expect and what you hold:
No real projects, dreams, or wants—
There's no need to come here now.

AMELIA
Daddy, I'm scared.

FATHER
He fell.

DODGE
Living is hard . . .

HELEN
Yes.

DODGE
. . . Dying isn't any better.

AMELIA
Not everything is possible?

FATHER
He seems to think he's flying.

DODGE
No.

HELEN
Yes.

AMELIA
You always meant the world to me,

And when you died, I lost my world.

A thousand times I wished for you,

At confirmation, graduation,

Recitals, plays, my wedding . . .

But no good-byes and do not cry . . .

I never even asked you how you died.

DODGE
Across the earth, at war, at sea,

I prayed each night for your welfare,

And lived for your letters, the
    pictures you drew:

"The Friendly Jungle," or the one

You sent of a girl on a swing

Inscribed "Amelia touches the sky."

I wasn't expecting you to die.

The risk?

The risk is worth the love?

A hand curled round your finger,

Tight as a frond,

The sweet breath of a sleeping baby.
The gentle weight of her head on
    your arm.

The risk?

The risk is worth the love.

The risk is worth the love.

HELEN
Lord, guard and guide all those who fly
Through the great spaces of the sky.

AMELIA
Daddy, you're wearing your dress
    whites—
Will there be a parade?

Be with them always in the air,

DODGE
I wore this to my change of
    command.

Remember?

In darkening storms

AMELIA
Yes, I do.

Or sunlight fair;

DODGE
Before I took the squadron back?

Oh, hear us when we lift our prayer

For those in peril in the air!

AMELIA
Before you died . . .

DODGE
Remember that horse you had as a child? I thought, how does this wisp
  of a girl control that enormous creature?

AMELIA
I just thought: this horse is like
  a plane.

DODGE
Let worry cease and fall away like
  shooting stars.

Are you going now?

Yes.

Is there somewhere you have to be?

DODGE *laughs, again.* AMELIA *reflexively touches her belly.*

Do you think I can control this enormous creature?

The risk is worth the love.

Okay.
I'll let you go now.

AMELIA *falls asleep as* DODGE *strokes her hair. The* FATHER *takes his son into
his arms and begins a wordless lament.*

HELEN
A testament to faith and power,

To dream of life, to give it birth —

FATHER, *vocalizes*

Each woman knows her strength on earth.

With will and heart she casts off fear
To soar into the atmosphere.

HELEN, *takes up the* FATHER's
wordless melody, smooths AMELIA's
blankets, kisses her on the forehead.

DODGE rises from the bed and
stations himself at its head.

FATHER
A testament to faith and power,
Creation in its finest hour,
YOUNG BOY
Father, don't leave me!

FATHER
To dream of flight, to leave the
earth,
Each flight an essay in rebirth.
YOUNG BOY
Father!
FATHER
I'm right here, son.

DODGE
A testament to faith and power,

Creation in its finest hour,

With will and heart he casts off fear
To soar into the atmosphere.
YOUNG BOY
Father, don't leave me!

A mission you cannot desert,
And life, like death, you can't rehearse.

DODGE *draws a letter from within his jacket and gently places it above*
AMELIA's *heart. He pulls the covers up over it, to her chin, and smooths them.*

I traded what was far for near:
I never meant to disappear.

DODGE crosses to exit past the YOUNG BOY. *As the* YOUNG BOY *repeats the cry of "Don't leave me!"* DODGE *pauses and observes compassionately, before continuing off.* HELEN *continues to comfort the father, the father comforts the* YOUNG BOY, *and the* YOUNG BOY *free-associates feverishly as* THE FLIER's *plane taxis through the wall.*

THE FLIER
A testament to faith and power,
Creation in its finest hour,
To have a dream, to know its worth
informs a life with weight and mirth.

THE FLIER taxis her plane to a stop.

Though obstacles, of course, appear,
You simply have to persevere.

THE FLIER, dressed in brown jodhpurs and ankle-high riding boots, with a crushed leather jacket that hits mid-thigh, a smooth caplike helmet, goggles, brown-and-white silk scarf tied at her neck, emerges from the cockpit, plants her hands on her hips, shakes the sleep out of her legs, and looks around, gazing at the space as if it were a beautiful place. HELEN *crosses to* AMELIA's *bed.*

THE FLIER
Maybe I'm not dead. Who knows?
What is important now is that I followed
my desire; I married the air—

I sat at the sun's feet; my lovers were the moon and the stars.
My time was my time, not wasted on fear,
or regret. And I was never bored.

PAUL enters.

PAUL, *to HELEN*
Any change?

HELEN shakes her head no as she hugs him hello. They embrace at length, and then PAUL goes to AMELIA's bedside and looks at her.

THE FLIER
I followed my dream to the end.

HELEN
Wake up, Amelia.

THE FLIER
And I didn't turn back.

PAUL
Wake up.

THE FLIER
I always said that if you start an adventure, you should see it through.

THE FLIER stands there, smiling brightly out at the world. The YOUNG BOY's heart monitor flat-lines. HELEN moves to and pushes the code-blue button, then immediately joins the FATHER. PAUL spins around to watch; the FATHER rises and leans over his son; the NURSE *and an* INTERN *run in. The* SECOND DOCTOR *appears. The frenzied business of resuscitation begins.*

FATHER
I swore I'd stay with him.

SECOND DOCTOR, *to the father*
You need to stand clear.

The paddles are triggered; there is no response. This happens three times.

Clear!

HELEN *takes the father aside. The resuscitation is abandoned. The music stops.* PAUL *yanks the curtains aside.*

FATHER
What's happening?

The SECOND DOCTOR *taps his watch.*

NURSE
6:04 p.m.

THE FLIER, *musing*
New beginnings.

The SECOND DOCTOR *looks up and sees* PAUL, *who has been observing them, and reflexively indicates to the* NURSE *and the* INTERN *that the boy's body should be removed. He nods to* PAUL *and pulls the curtains closed as the*

NURSE and intern wheel the bed out of the room. The SECOND DOCTOR *exits.* HELEN *leads the* FATHER *out. During the following aria,* THE FLIER *turns very slowly in place, surveying her surroundings.* PAUL *wheels back to look at* AMELIA's *bed, then moves back to it, frantic for her to wake up. He moves his hands over her bedclothes, vaguely tucking her in and straightening the sheets and her hair, perhaps touching her face as he murmurs associatively, sometimes very adamant, even possibly angry, sometimes pleading, urging, kissing her.*

PAUL
Please . . . my angel . . . wake up. Come back . . . are the pillows okay? . . . Our baby needs you. It's hard to face the fear . . . the risk . . . I've just come back . . . I understand . . . don't leave me to raise her alone . . . there's some water here . . . I need you. Listen . . .

PAUL stops suddenly as his hands happen upon something under the sheet, It is the letter burned by the Vietnamese couple, written by DODGE *before his last mission.*

(*Reading the letter*)
    My two loves,

    The Grim Reaper called today.
    It's "go" on the Haiphong power plant.
    I am leading eight planes and fully expect

    Heavy opposition. I am at peace within myself.
    I have no fear, but write this for reality's sake.
    If I am shot down and should eject,

Please know I will bear whatever lies ahead.
If I am lost, do not despair.
Keep faith; go forward; never forget

How thankful I am and how happy you have made me.
You deserve everything good in life, especially love,
So leave the doors open.

I love you always,
Dodge

The father enters a waiting room stage right, accompanied by HELEN. *They sit down together, remain silent.* PAUL *examines the letter, turns it over, folds it, and holds it in his hand, thinking.*

THE FLIER
If I am lost, do not despair.
I have a good feeling about this place,
whatever it is.
One lives on,
quite in spite of circumstances.

The DOCTOR *enters* AMELIA's *room.* PAUL *rises as the* DOCTOR *checks* AMELIA's *chart and monitor.*

THE FLIER
We don't really have a choice.

The DOCTOR *and* PAUL *are seen beginning to converse, but we don't hear them. A* PRIEST *enters the waiting room with a plastic bag containing the*

YOUNG BOY's valuables and greets the FATHER *and* HELEN, *but we don't hear them. The* FATHER, HELEN, *and the* PRIEST *continue a subdued conversation during the following. The* FATHER *clutches the bag of valuables.*

THE FLIER
I can hear them
talking about me.
They're bound to.
Wondering what I'm up to,
through the great spaces of the sky.

DOCTOR
A C-section is the safest choice.

THE FLIER, *wryly*
Full of opinions . . .

PAUL
But if she wakes up, and all her signs are good . . .

DOCTOR
We don't know how stable she is after three days out.

THE FLIER
One thing's for sure, I've never felt so alive.

PAUL
She would die if she couldn't do it herself.

DOCTOR
She could die if she tried.

AMELIA
Who said anything about dying?

PAUL, *pocketing the letter*
Angel . . .

PAUL and the DOCTOR fly to AMELIA's side.

AMELIA
It's natural childbirth or I get another doctor.
What time is it? God, I slept well.

DOCTOR
This isn't safe.

AMELIA
I passed out in your office, didn't I?

(*To PAUL*)
You must have been *beside* yourself.

DOCTOR
This isn't safe.
You've been unconscious for three days.

AMELIA
I know. I couldn't help overhearing.

(*Tries to sit up*)
I'm sorry, Doctor.
I appreciate your concern, but—
I feel kind of weird—

PAUL, *reflexively moving to her*
Honey, let me help you.

DOCTOR
I really feel that . . .

AMELIA
Ah!

DOCTOR
I feel that you shouldn't . . .

AMELIA
Ah!

PAUL AND AMELIA
Oh, my God, I . . .

DOCTOR
I have to advise—given the circumstances—
that we—

AMELIA, *to the DOCTOR*
No. No Cesarean. Period.
I can do this.

THE FLIER *smiles.* PAUL *follows. During the transition to the final scene, a* GRIEF COUNSELOR *enters the waiting room and shakes hands with the* FATHER, *converses with him and the* PRIEST, *but we do not hear them.* HELEN *exits the waiting room. The stage gradually reassembles into a layout identical to act 1, scene 1: a room stage right (the waiting room /* YOUNG AMELIA's *bedroom), a room stage left (the birthing room / the kitchen of the old house). There is a hallway running upstage and downstage between them, and a long, narrow space running across the downstage area, stage left to stage right (a hallway with some waiting-room furniture / the porch of the old house). There is a scrubbing-in room downstage left, attached to the birthing room. Dividing walls are either scrim or absent.*

ACT 2 / SCENE 3

AMELIA is on a birthing bed, which is seen through a scrim. She is in the throes of labor, attended by PAUL, NURSES, and INTERNS, all in scrubs. Over on the other side of the stage, the PRIEST exits the waiting room, leaving the FATHER with the GRIEF COUNSELOR. The DOCTOR and HELEN stand in the scrubbing-in room, in scrubs.

DOCTOR
Do you think you could say something?

HELEN
She's been in labor for six hours, and she's absolutely determined.

DOCTOR
I have to advise against this.
You know there is a risk.

HELEN
Well, maybe the risk is worth it.
It's her body, and it's what she wants.

HELEN moves to the door of the birthing room, turns back at the door.

DOCTOR
There is a danger—

HELEN
It's not your decision to make.
Let's go.

HELEN opens the door of the birthing room and holds it for the DOCTOR, who follows her in.

THE FLIER crosses to the stage left waiting area, sits, picks up a magazine, leafs through it, as if waiting for news to come.

The GRIEF COUNSELOR exits the waiting room, leaves the FATHER alone.

PAUL moves to the door and into the scrubbing-in room, leans against the wall, slightly dazed, takes a huge breath and lets it out, thinks a moment, goes back into the birthing room.

A NURSE crosses from stage left to stage right in the downstage hall.

The FATHER reaches into the plastic bag and takes out his son's wallet, opens it, looks at it a moment, then puts it back in the plastic bag.

THE FLIER rises and paces, stage right, restless.

*At the moment that the baby is delivered and held aloft, the orchestra stops.
The company sings a brilliantly pulsating, joyous* quodlibet *of themes from the
opera. As they sing, the baby is cleaned up and* AMELIA *is settled back into the
bed. The* DOCTOR *lays the baby in* AMELIA's *arms. The* DOCTOR, INTERNS,
and NURSES *leave.* HELEN *sits on a chair and weeps for joy.* PAUL *remains
with* AMELIA *and the baby. The actors who portrayed* YOUNG AMELIA,
AMANDA, *and* DODGE *return as a* NURSE, *a* SECOND NURSE, *and a* THIRD
DOCTOR.

THE FLIER
And I was never bored.

HELEN
Da Vinci said there shall be wings.

NURSE (YOUNG AMELIA)
To soar into the atmosphere!

AMELIA
Anything is possible up in the stars . . .

SECOND NURSE (AMANDA)
A feather pushed up by the wind.

THIRD DOCTOR (DODGE)
You can't imagine how happy she'll make you.

PAUL
The risk is worth the love!

DOCTOR
Creation in its finest hour!

FATHER
It's not like anything I ever knew.

Gradually, voices drop out as characters exit, leaving the THIRD DOCTOR and PAUL, whose parts are featured above THE FLIER and AMELIA. Presently, only AMELIA and THE FLIER are left singing. As THE FLIER enters the birthing room and stands apart, the FATHER stands up and moves to the door of the hallway. He stops to put on his coat.

THE FLIER
And I was never bored.

AMELIA
Anything is possible . . .
Hi, baby.

The FATHER walks slowly up the long center hallway and out of the hospital; AMELIA and PAUL caress the baby while HELEN looks on from her chair. THE FLIER stands looking out thoughtfully as the lights fade to black.

END OF THE OPERA

For me, the first hint of *Amelia* began one spring afternoon in 2004, when Daron Hagen called to ask if I'd like to write a libretto for an opera he wanted to compose on the subject of flight. The libretto would be a lyric sequence of poems, and he was reading a book by Tom D. Crouch, *Wings: A History of Aviation from Kites to the Space Age*, which he recommended. I didn't hesitate. My father had been a 1950 graduate of the United States Naval Academy, trained in flight school at Naval Air Station Pensacola, was later an instructor at the air station at Whiting Field; his father, also an academy graduate, had been a pilot and test pilot; and many of my poems are preoccupied with flight. The subject felt close to home. Daron had set my poem "Sonnet" to music in 1984 at Yaddo, the upstate New York artists' colony where we'd met, and I admired his music. Although an opera neo-phyte, I was intrigued by the libretto form, which struck me as being close to poetry in its concision, use of imagery and repetition, occasional high lyric mode, and dramatic monologue, an analogue in my mind to aria and scena. I suspected I would be able to explore emotions and thoughts that had not yet found a way into poems. I was eager for the adventure of collaboration. And so we set out.

Daron pitched eight different opera scenarios to Speight Jenkins, general director of Seattle Opera, before they settled on one Daron called "Flight Music," in which Leonardo da Vinci, Icarus, Daedalus, Orville and Wilbur Wright, Neil Armstrong, a young girl, and Thomas Ferebee, the bombardier who released the first atomic bomb, were characters. When Speight asked Daron to strengthen the opera's through story, eliminating the idea of a lyric sequence, he suggested Daron speak with Stephen Wadsworth, who had already directed several productions for Seattle Opera and, a decade earlier, the first production of Daron's *Shining Brow*.

In the course of their work together, Daron brought up the details of my life and suggested they might be able to adapt my biography to serve as the through story of the opera. They had both read my book of poems, *The Pilot's Daughter*, and Seattle Opera had agreed to sign me on as librettist on the basis of this volume. The book is an elegy for my father, who served in Vietnam from November 1965 to mid-June 1966 aboard the USS *Enterprise* (CVN-65), flying more than one hundred bombing missions and earning two Distinguished Flying Crosses and twelve air medals. On a rainy night in December 1966, during training operations off California, his plane went down in the Pacific after a catapult shot off the *Bon Homme Richard*. He was commanding officer of VA-76, readying the squadron for a second tour in the Gulf of Tonkin. He was never recovered. My mother was thirty-eight; I was fourteen, my brother nine. The poems in my book deal with that loss, its repercussions, and the sequence of their arrangement moves from death to life, from the loss of my father to the birth of my daughter, by way of a lot of unanswered questions, grief, and ambivalence.

By September 2004, Stephen had turned Daron's early treatment into a two-act story, titled "Amelia," featuring elements from my poems and life but revised and developed for dramatic effect. It concerned the protagonist, Amelia, on the verge of giving birth, still steeped in the grief and ambivalence engendered by her father's disappearance and death when she was a child. Her father, like my father, was a pilot who fought in the Vietnam War. Her father, like my father, was irretrievably lost, but under different circumstances. A key image in the story (the open door) derives from the poem "Missing" in my book: "I have kept / all the doors open in my life / so that he could walk in. . . . " Elements carried forward from Daron's original treatment include the expressionistic use of mythological and historical figures to embody the protagonist's inner world. New story elements include the trip Amelia and her mother take to Vietnam, with a flashback of the pilot's capture, and her three-day lapse into unconsciousness, during which she dreams herself back to health before giving birth.

In May 2005, Daron and I visited Yaddo to work. He was trying out musical ideas for the opera by composing "Flight Music," a song cycle using Amelia Earhart's words for text, and I was writing poems out of my own fascination with Earhart and new thoughts about my father. Daron set one small lyric, "Amelia's Song," to music. That music now begins the opera. Some of the words from another poem I worked on at the time ("The Vow") turn up in the Flier's words in act 2, scene 2: "I married the air—I sat at the sun's feet; my lovers were the moon and stars." We spent time talking about the opera, its thematic concerns, and the images that might signal those themes and recur throughout: light/stars/ birds, freedom/flight/dream, fear/death/birth. I asked him if he might find a way to allude to the Navy Hymn, "Eternal Father, Strong to Save"; he ultimately used it as the basis for the set of variations that underpin the action of act 2, scene 2. I was also reading a lot of librettos, though I soon came to feel that reading others' work, while interesting and pleasurable, was a stalling mechanism that kept me from producing my own.

We did not begin in earnest until May 2006, again at Yaddo. By that time, we had contracts with Seattle Opera and a final, mutually agreeable scenario in hand. Also, by that time, I was versed in opera terminology and what would be an underlying principle for my work: every minute of text would result in approximately three minutes of music, a neat formula that might sound constricting but proved liberating, the way any formal structure, paradoxically, can liberate the working poet. As the scenario reflected time sequence as well as action, I knew the parameters of my project.

Each morning, I sat down at my computer in Yaddo's High Studio to write, using the scenario as an outline but feeling free to invent key imagery to associate with the characters and to supply emotional motivation for their actions. When I completed a scene, I would share it with Daron, who processed the text by retyping it, sometimes making a deletion or asking for an additional line or two. If he saw something I'd written that might make "a nice little arietta," he'd point it out. One such instance resulted in Amelia's arietta in act 1, scene 2, which begins: "Why think of the blue canary I had at six?" In other words, he saw what I was doing; he took what had potential from his perspective and urged me to develop it. He cheered me when I got something "on the mark" and caught me when I went too much toward what we both called "poetry land." This place was usually characterized by excessive description or dialogue that didn't ring true to how we imagined our characters would talk. Sometimes he'd say, "We need a duet here," and that would become my next project in High Studio, which more than once, with its boxy shape and aerial view of the sweeping lawn, fountain, and distant trees, felt like a cockpit.

Working in a new genre can be frightening, especially when dealing with personal material. Daron's gift to me, aside from the invitation to collaborate, was in granting me what he called "moral authority" in writing the libretto. He was a patient teacher in all opera-related matters, forthright and supportive as I reached into the unknown for the unknown. He would laugh when I'd say, "I don't want to write doggerel," and hand him stanzas of rhyming iambic tetrameter, a metrical form I don't normally adopt. Early on in the process when I was agonizing over beginning, I told him I had dreamed about dead blue jays. Daron said, "Put it in the opera," and a novelist in residence at the time said the dream suggested rebirth. In the libretto, Amelia tells her husband about a dream of dead blue jays (which she thinks signals her fear of flight and death), but her husband counters with "That dream is about rebirth."

By the time I left Yaddo in mid-June, I had finished the first two scenes of act 1. They contained memories and images from my childhood; a quote from Edna St. Vincent Millay's "God's World," which I'd memorized in third grade; young Amelia's apostrophe to the stars, inspired by my school's assembly processional hymn ("The Spacious Firmament on High"); a lullaby informed by my love of W. H. Auden's "Lullaby"; and a free verse poem in the voice of Amelia Earhart, imagined as she approaches the end of her fatal 1937 round-the-world flight, written at Yaddo the year before. I could not begin scene 3 because it was set in Vietnam, and, in an Oscar Wildean twist, I was about to experience the truth of his claim "Life imitates art." Like Amelia and her mother, who visit Vietnam to learn what happened to their lost father/husband, I was going with my husband to Vietnam, a place I never thought I would travel to or, indeed, want to visit—to learn what? My father had been dead for more than forty years. His plane lay on the Pacific floor. I told myself I wanted to see the colors and texture of the landscape. I wanted to breathe the air and meet the people. I wanted to hear the Vietnamese language.

* * *

On September 12, my husband and I flew to Hanoi for a twelve-day tour of sites in Vietnam that recalled the American war. Our plan was to start in the north and work our way south to Ho Chi Minh City, formerly Saigon. During the nineteen-hour trip, I reread Michael Herr's *Dispatches* and David Lamb's *Vietnam Now*. Other books had also contributed to my thinking about the libretto, among them, Jim Stockdale's *In Love and War*, William Lawrence's *Tennessee Patriot*, and John McCain's *Faith of Our Fathers*. My feelings veered between elation at the prospect of seeing a new part of the world and fear inspired by my associations with it. Should I even be traveling there at all? I heard my deceased mother uttering an emphatic "No." She would never have dreamed of visiting the country my father had fought against and, in the United States' misguided conflict, sacrificed his life for. How to square what he suffered as a pilot on the line in the Tonkin Gulf, where the sortie schedule was grueling, the temperatures unbearably hot, the carrier quarters cramped, with my plans for research and sightseeing? It felt surreal.

As documented in Lamb's book, American veterans were the first to make contact with Vietnam after Saigon fell and before the United States opened up trade relations there. They went back to find closure and make peace with what had happened. I wondered if the daughter of a veteran could find closure or peace. I had read the more than three hundred pages of letters my father had written to my mother during his deployment in Vietnam. Parts of his four "last" letters, those written to loved ones for distribution only in the event of death, are telescoped in the letter aria in act 2, scene 2. I knew that as early as the fall of 1965, when he arrived in Vietnam, he felt that the United States would never "win" the war as it was being prosecuted by Washington. Our failings from the outset, in misjudging the "enemy" and being ignorant of Vietnamese history, are old news. Yet how sad and sobering to think that as early as 1965, men fighting there knew the endeavor was doomed. Only honor and, as the pilot explains to his daughter in the first scene of *Amelia*, "a duty to the men in my squadron" kept them at their posts.

We approached Hanoi through cirrus clouds and a fine mist covering the earth. It was still monsoon season, and 91 degrees. I was touching down two months shy of forty-one years after my father had arrived there, he by aircraft carrier and I by Singapore Airlines. What would he have thought of my trip? Suddenly the coast and Tonkin Bay appeared. The wide Red River looked aptly named; it was red as dried blood, and the vernal squares of rice paddies in the delta were beautiful from the sky, just like my father had described to us.

In Hanoi, we visited Ho Chi Minh's Mausoleum and house, a humble contrast to the garish, imperial Reunification Palace (formerly president Ngo Dinh Diem's Independence Palace) in Ho Chi Minh City. We saw Hoa Lo

Prison, better known as the Hanoi Hilton, where U.S. pilots were incarcerated, and drove to Truc Bach Lake, where John McCain was shot down in October 1967. We toured the Army Museum, which proved invaluable for learning about uniforms, artillery, and airplanes. Although Vietnam today is capitalistic and modernized, with much of it rebuilt (save large portions of the still deforested DMZ and the unusable mined countryside), I asked to see a North Vietnamese village that might have existed in the mid-1960s. I wanted to root my imagination in real soil.

Our guide took us to Duong Lam in Ha Tay province, about two hours outside Hanoi. This became the setting for act 1, scene 3, complete with the communal house and rice stalks spread out in the square for drying. In Duong Lam, we visited two families, one of whom lived in the oldest house, dating back twelve generations. From them I learned that during the war, several pilots shot down in the vicinity were kept in a building, long since destroyed, until they could be transported to Hoa Lo Prison. All along the road back to Hanoi, we saw rice fields, with women wearing *non la*, or conical hats, bent over, working as they have done for hundreds of years or walking along the road with baskets of pink lotus flowers.

On another day, we traveled to Ha Long Bay and drove back by way of Haiphong, one of the world's best deepwater harbors, the harbor the United States would not mine until the end of the war but repeatedly asked our pilots to traverse on bombing missions, often resulting in their demise or capture. My father received a Distinguished Flying Cross for leading an alpha strike on a thermal power plant in the area. We passed through Uong Bi, where, according to our guide, the first documented American pilot was shot down: Everett Alvarez. Hanoi's Army Museum displays a picture of him upon capture being led away from the "carcass" of his plane.

From Hanoi, we traveled to Hue, which was seized by the North Vietnamese during the Tet Offensive, the DMZ along the seventeenth parallel, and the Vinh Moc tunnel complex in Quang Tri province, which functioned from 1965 to 1973 as an underground base and passageway from which North Vietnamese embarked to fight and carry supplies to the south. We took Highway 1 to Da Nang, traversing the Hai Van Pass. We stopped at the pass where U.S. forces had occupied a "gateway" outpost during the war. Our guide pointed to the adjacent green hillside overlooking Da Nang. "Over there was the Ho Chi Minh Trail," he said matter-of-factly. This was a target, my father wrote, that U.S. pilots repeatedly bombed to no effect.

At China Beach, in Ho Chi Minh City, in the Cu Chi Tunnels, and along the Mekong River, there were myriad sights to contemplate; overall, the trip was as illuminating as it was sad. I had gathered the concrete details I needed for the libretto. I knew where the pilot would eject; I knew the kind of village he would land in; I knew what his captors would wear and what they would say. I also discovered the truth of what former POW Vice Admiral William Lawrence had written in *Tennessee Patriot*, "Under any other circumstances [than those of war] the Vietnamese are an inherently gentle people." What had we done to them? What had we done to ourselves?

One of my observations on one of our last days was how nationalism pervades the country: Vietnam's red flag with its central gold star flies from the flag tower of Hue's Citadel and from Ho Chi Minh's tomb in Hanoi as well as from the lowliest home along the river. It flies from government buildings and fishing boats, new construction sites and memorial cemeteries. I would not have been surprised to see it flying from a water buffalo's tail. The flag insisted on making its way into the stage directions.

* * *

Although the pilot/father passes out of the story's action early and what we later see of him occurs in flashback as the Vietnamese couple recount their story to Amelia and her mother, he returns in act 2, scene 2, in Amelia's dream. Because my recollection and perception of my father were those of a fourteen-year-old, I wanted to interview other pilots who had known him as an adult and a colleague. I wanted to know about life on a carrier, which, when he was alive, was still an entirely male bastion. This had a bearing on the kind of man the character in the opera would be. Before going to Vietnam, in the spring and summer of 2006, I made three trips, the first to the Smithsonian Institution's National Air and Space Museum in Washington, D.C. There I saw, to my surprise, a replica of the USS *Enterprise*, the world's first nuclear-powered aircraft carrier, commissioned in 1961. My father was deployed on it in 1965 when it became the first nuclear-powered carrier used in war.

I learned about the small floating city that a carrier is. I learned how planes were launched—by a steam-driven catapult, capable of accelerating an eighty-thousand-pound aircraft like my father's to 160 miles per hour from a standstill, able to launch an airplane every fifteen seconds at the start of a mission. Clearly, one had to be fit, mentally acute, and confident to take to the air this way. Returning to the carrier, which from the air was the size of a postage stamp on the ocean, was even harder, especially at night. As a pilot says in the documentary *Fighter Pilot*: "Putting twenty tons of airplane down on a pitching deck and wire will get adrenaline flowing in the veins of the most experienced pilot." In a small gallery adjacent to the carrier model hung a Douglas A-4 Skyhawk (the plane my father flew), emblazoned with the name of my father's executive officer, who took command of VA-76 after my father died: Byron Fuller. He was shot down over North Vietnam on his last mission in July 1967, six months after his deployment there, and held in the Hanoi Hilton until the war ended.

I went to Florida to talk to him. Admiral Fuller shared an entire afternoon with me, answering questions about my father as well as about his own shoot-down, capture, imprisonment, and torture. His wife did not know if he was alive for the first two years after he was taken prisoner. What kept him going were thoughts of his family. He thought about his son's sports, his daughter's dancing lessons. He did not mention faith, but he said the men in the squadron who had faith, like my father, tended not to talk about it. Those without faith talked about it all the time. I asked him what my father's mind-set had been going back for a second tour of duty in Vietnam. He said loyalty to the men was a huge factor in my father's thinking. His view was: "I have a job to do and I'm going to do it." We ranged over many topics dealing with the war; he showed me the itinerary and photographs of his recent trip to Vietnam. Though he didn't tell me this at the time, I learned later that out of the 147 repatriated naval officer POWs, four were awarded the Navy Cross; one of them was Byron. When he walked me to my car, he said: "Let me know how your man turns out. God bless you."

My third trip was to Pensacola, the "Cradle of Naval Aviation," to meet and stay with Admiral Richard Gaskill and his wife, Diane. My brother met me there, and together we toured the National Museum of Naval Aviation and the air station where the museum resides. Ensigns go from Annapolis to Pensacola for flight training school. My father would have been there in 1951. From Admiral Gaskill I learned many terms and definitions—what rolling in and pulling off a target means and the need during that time to keep your wingman in sight. I learned what a vertical roll is, an arresting cable, a stick, gyro, T-bar, ordnance, LSO, CAG, an alpha strike. Why do pilots fly? I asked. "The better you get, the more part of the air you feel" was his answer. Admiral Fuller had answered similarly: "For the exhilaration of it."

Admiral Gaskill first met my father in 1956, and they remained close friends. He attended the change of command at the naval air station in Lemoore, California, in the fall of 1966, when my father became commanding officer of VA-76. Admiral Gaskill was executive commanding officer of the USS *Enterprise* at the end of the war, participating in the heavy December 1972 bombing that led to the January cease-fire and carrying home forty POWs. At his house, the admiral produced a 1950 annual register of the Naval Academy, pointing out that my father's highest marks were in aptitude and leadership, followed by English and French. He graduated from the Naval Academy at twenty-three; fifteen years later he would be in combat; in another year, dead. If you're trained to do something, you're going to do it, Admiral Fuller had said. My father, like the pilot in *Amelia*, trained to fly in war; when called to serve, he went.

By the time I started work again on the libretto in October 2006, I had a better sense of who the pilot/husband/father figure was. He was based on memories of my father but informed by my interviews with Admirals Gaskill and Fuller. Each man exemplified courage, honor, and duty, strength, faith, and willingness to make the ultimate sacrifice. My father had paid that sacrifice, like the pilot in *Amelia*.

From October to December, I finished the libretto in New York City, meeting regularly with Daron to resume our collaboration. I continued to weave bits of relevant verse into the text: Robert Louis Stevenson's "The Swing," which my grandmother used to recite to me, and Herman Melville's "The March into Virginia Ending in the First Manassas." I used lines from some of my earlier poems and, again, memories from childhood. In January, we met multiple times with Stephen to work through the manuscript, which I revised for concision and dramatic tension. One of the features of a viable libretto is its skeletal nature, which the music fleshes out.

* * *

Now it is May 2007, and Daron and I are again at Yaddo. He is in the Tower, writing the music for *Amelia* at the same piano where Marc Blitzstein wrote *Regina*. We meet for afternoon conversations; he sings and plays what he has written, and it is a joy to hear how the characters "sound," how their story will soar. The first music he wrote for the opera was the letter aria in act 2, scene 2, because we felt this moment was the most powerful and highly charged. "If I can get the tone here," he told me, "we'll be okay." At Daron's request, I asked my brother to send me a snapshot of my father climbing out of the cockpit of his plane. When I showed it to Daron, he said, "Yes, I think we've got the beginning of him. Now we can go forward."

He asks me specific questions about who I think the most significant characters are ("Who do we care about most after Amelia?") and where their key emotional moments occur. He asks how I think a character might react in a given situation, because all of this will inform the music. At breakfast one morning, he inquired how I thought Amelia might manifest anger and frustration; that afternoon, he played and sang for me the first draft of her climactic act 2 scena.

Though the premiere is three years off as I write this, the libretto is finished, except for the occasional word added or subtracted to fit the needs of musicalization. What began as a professional engagement turned into a spiritual and imaginative journey. I gleaned much from my research and travel that doesn't appear overtly in the libretto but serves, I hope, in the background, to lend it emotional, historical truth and resonance. I call *Amelia* a "psychological" opera; Daron calls it "expressionistic." Maybe it's both, tracing as it does the outward trajectory of the protagonist's inner drama.

Sometimes I think my work will have been to conjure my father back, to stand on the stage and sing—not just to me, but to anyone who has fought or lost a loved one in service to his or her country, and to every parent or child. As Leonardo da Vinci wrote, in lines that greet the visitor to Seattle's Museum of Flight, which I was fortunate to tour with its president, Dr. Bonnie Dunbar: "There shall be wings: the spirit cannot die."

Therein lies the miracle to outlast war and death.

Yaddo
May 28–31, 2007

ACKNOWLEDGMENTS

I wish to thank those who provided information, support, and advice during the research and compositional stages of the libretto: Dr. Bonnie Dunbar, president and director of the Museum of Flight in Seattle; Rear Admiral and Mrs. Richard T. Gaskill, USN (Ret.); Rear Admiral and Mrs. Byron Fuller, USN (Ret.); Cristina Alfar; Alice Attie; John Balaban; Corinna Clendenen; Anita Fore; Susan Goodrich; Cynde Iverson; Bruce Johnson; Dr. Anita LaSala; Gilda Lyons; Susan Miller; Trang-mai Ngo; Phuong Nguyen; Trang-thu Nguyen; Stephanie Rudy; and Hazel Shanken. For their help and enthusiasm in publishing the libretto, I am grateful to Pat Soden, director of the University of Washington Press; Marilyn Trueblood, managing editor; Laura Iwasaki, copyeditor; and Ashley Saleeba, senior designer.

My deep gratitude as well to Seattle Opera's general director Speight Jenkins, for his confidence and generosity; to Seattle Opera's administrative director, Kelly Tweeddale; and to my collaborators, Daron Hagen and Stephen Wadsworth, whose talent I admire and whose friendship I've been lucky to enjoy. During May 2008, Seattle Opera, with funds from Opera America, sponsored a workshop for the opera, which was invaluable in terms of hearing the words set to music from beginning to end. My thanks to Maestro Gerard Schwarz, Phil Kelsey, David McDade, Jocelyn Dueck, Kendra Johnson, Cay Q. Bach, Clare Burovac, the singers who participated in the workshop, and Seattle Opera's patrons. I am grateful, finally and significantly, to my husband, Peter Olberg; my daughter, Amanda Olberg; my brother and sister-in-law, Dodge and Mimi McFall; and Yaddo, that special place, presided over by Elaina Richardson, benevolent president, and Candace Wait, wizard program director. Yaddo afforded me the time and room in which to make this inward flight and gathered the artists who, during my residencies there (and sometimes after), whether they knew it or not, contributed to my work with their insights and interest: Tom Cipullo, Eric Lane, Antonia Logue, Henrietta Mantooth, Tanya Selvaratnam, James Siena, and Susan Unterberg. At the start of my 2006 residency at Yaddo, I asked a fellow guest, Michael Tilson Thomas, what advice he would give a first-time librettist. He said: "Write words the singers can sing!" I hope I have done that.

ABOUT THE AUTHOR

Librettist Gardner McFall was born in Jacksonville, Florida. She received a B.A. from Wheaton College in Massachusetts, an M.A. in the Writing Seminars from The Johns Hopkins University, and a Ph.D. in English from New York University. A poet by trade, Ms. McFall's poems have appeared widely, in such publications as *The Atlantic Monthly, Southwest Review, Paris Review, Seattle Review, The Nation, Missouri Review* (where she won the Thomas McAfee prize for poetry), and *The New Yorker*. She received a "Discovery"/*The Nation* award in 1989. Her first book of poems, *The Pilot's Daughter* (1996), was an elegy for her father, who was lost at sea in training operations for his second tour of duty in Vietnam. Her second collection, *Russian Tortoise*, has recently been published. Ms. McFall is the author of two children's books, the editor of *Made with Words*, a prose miscellany by May Swenson, and the author of the introduction and notes for a new edition of Kenneth Grahame's *The Wind in the Willows*. She teaches at Hunter College and lives in New York City with her husband and daughter.

Photo by Susan Unterberg